W9-AOR-423

BEAR WHO DARES

KATE TOMS

Castle
Street
PRESS

If **YOU** were a bear,

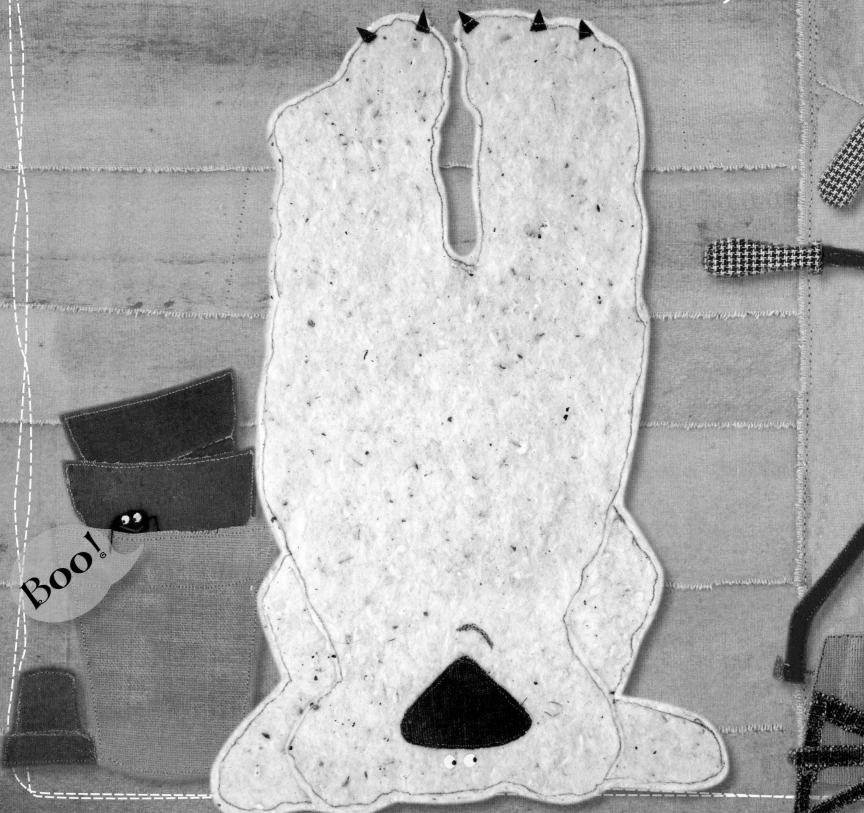

Boo!

would you dare

to stand on

your head

in the

shed?

Would **you** leave your **bed**

and
sleep
underneath
it
instead?

Would you slurp
sticky honey

through a straw?

Honey

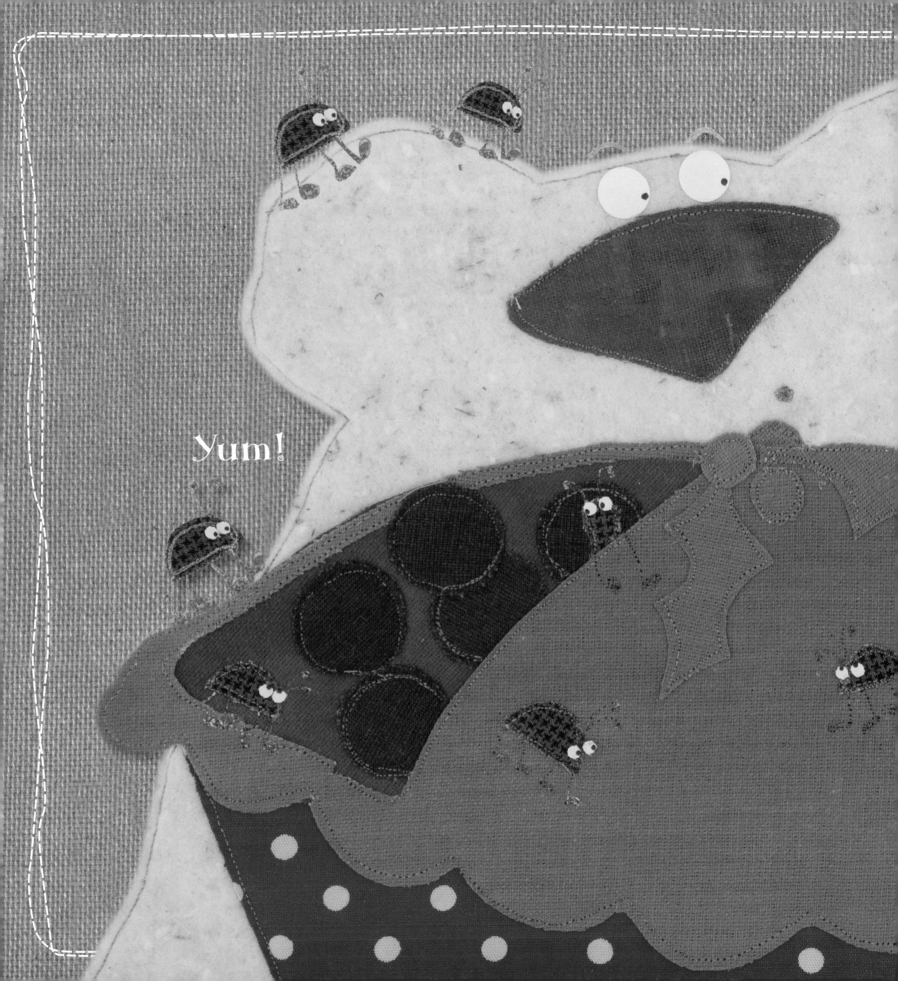

Yum!

Or eat beetle pies with your paw?

Yum!

Yum!

If you were a bear, would you dare

Would
you
wear
your
clothes

one size fits all.

Dry Clean Only

back
to
front
and
inside
out?

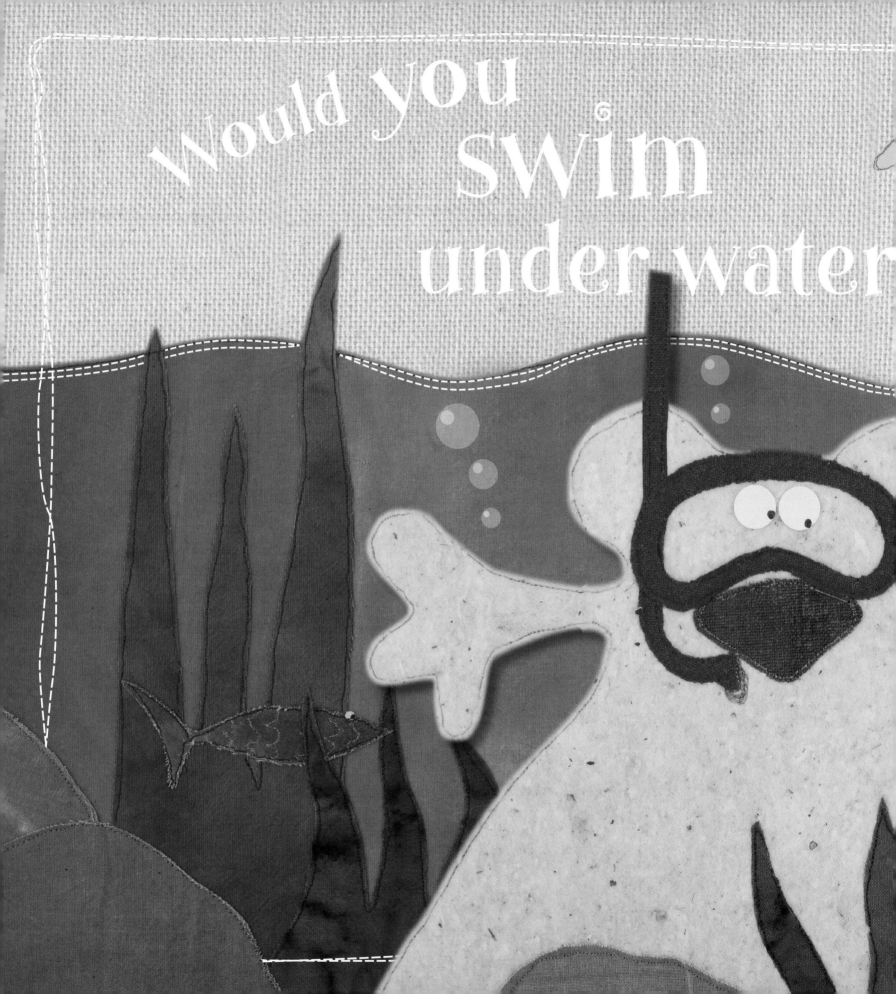

Would you swim under water?

and fly through the skies?

If **you** were a **bear**, would **you** dare

to go **out** without **combing** your **hair?**

Would you put on a **mask** and give dad a **scare?**

Or would you do
wheelies,

your feet
in the air?

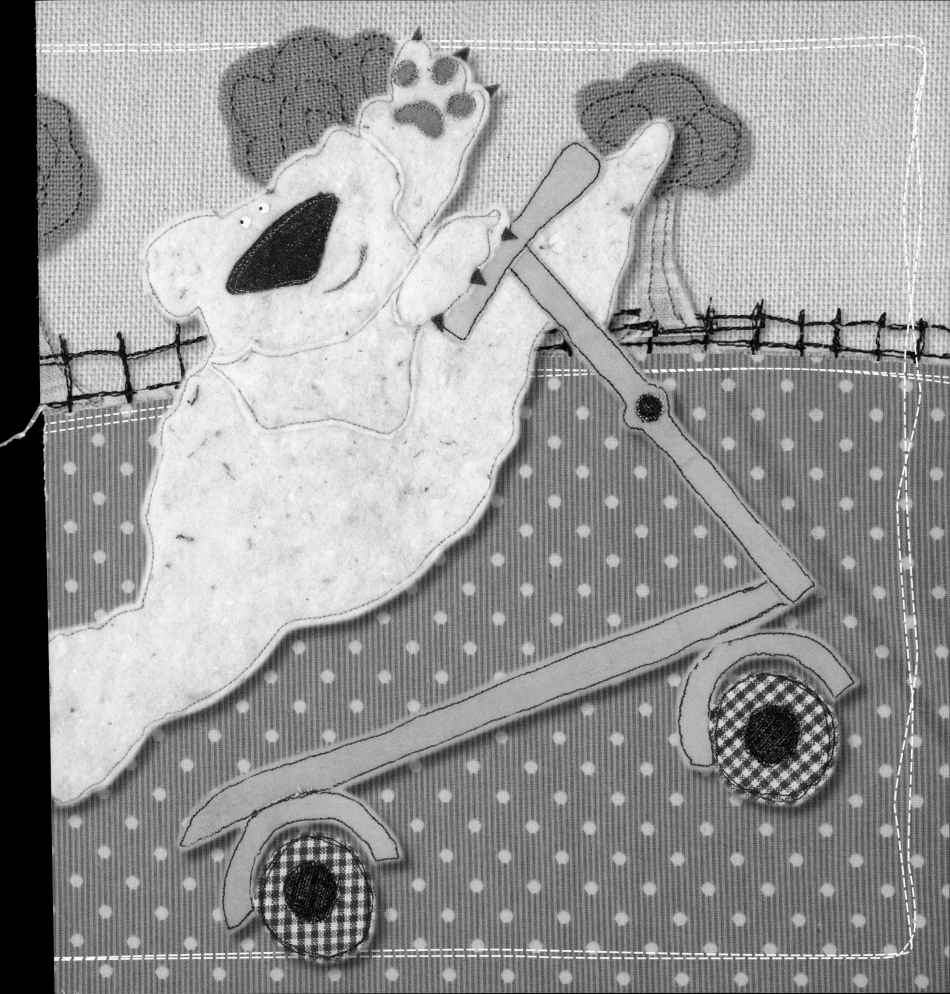